The Hidden Cove:
Pirate's Misadventure

BY

CELINKA SERRE

COVER BY
BINKY INK

BINKY INK

THE LITERARY ARM OF BINKY PRODUCTIONS

WWW.BINKYPRODUCTIONS.COM/SHORTSTORIES

<u>WARNINGS:</u>

Strong Language, Mature Subject Matter,
Blood, Violence, Vomiting.

Table of Contents

PART ONE

A storm raged outside the cabin, levin alighting the night sky. Edmund slapped the map on the table, pressing down for balance as the ship rocked. He passed his hand along the trail he was following. It had to be the right path – *he* had to be on the right path.

He'd studied his father's journals diligently, the man had left no doubt as to where the Hidden Cove should be.

Edmund's signet ring gleamed brighter than all the thirteen others that adorned his fingers, catching the candlelight from the shaking chandelier above him. It was the ring his father had bestowed upon him in his final moments before his death – upon *him*. The burden felt heavy, to be obliged to carry out his father's mission.

'Why me, though?' Edmund asked himself aloud, as he strove to quell his trembling hands. 'Why only me?'

It was the beliefs his father had instilled in him, to obey his orders, to seek his pride, that drove Edmund forward in this. It was how his father had survived. The man had been a Royal Navy officer. The irony was his father had failed to obey one single order, an order that had saved many lives. He, along with those he'd saved, had been deemed a deserter and would have been tried and hanged.

'If you don't follow orders, you may not survive, but if you follow them blindly, you might lose yourself, and without yourself, you cannot survive for very long.' Those words his father had repeated countless times.

Edmund's father and his crew had left to become pirates, and the man had earned his Captain's title once he'd learnt all about being a pirate from the captain who had taken him and his crew in.

Now, having been raised to obey with enough discernment to know when not to, Edmund was carrying out his father's wishes – his dying wishes. His father had chosen *Edmund* as his successor, and Edmund had promised his dying father he would see this mission to completion.

He chose you over me, just like he always did! William's voice rang out in Edmund's mind.

Edmund closed his eyes at the memory, the scene playing out once more.

* * *

'He didn't choose me over you, William.'

'Yes, he did, and you know it. He made *you* Captain of the ship. Not me, not us – you. He didn't believe I could do it, he never believed in me – I've always been in your shadow, Edmund!'

'Do you think I wanted this? I don't want to have to carry out father's mission. Do you know how many ships never return from that cove? He's sending me to my death!'

'Then why do you carry out father's wishes?' William demanded.

'Because I honour him.'

'That's what separates us, brother,' William seethed. 'He never honoured *us* – only ordered us about while we slaved away on his ship, lesser than the rest of his crew, yet *we were his sons*! I'm not sailing to my death, Edmund. Consider yourself one crewman short.'

William backed away from Edmund.

'What, you're leaving? Just like that?' cried Edmund.

'No, not just like that. I do not take this decision lightly, brother, but I have to. I will *not* give my life to some asinine fantasy just because father was obsessed with a legend.'

And William had turned his back on Edmund and the *Charmed Trove* . . . and walked away.

They had not spoken since. It had been three years.

* * *

The ship teetered – Edmund's stomach lurched. He was afraid, afraid he had made a mistake in pursuing his father's dream . . . Or was William correct that it was an obsession?

Edmund rolled up the map and slid it into its glass casing. He secured the cylinder on his belt and left his cabin, bounding to the deck.

'Captain, land ho!'

Excitement made Edmund's heart race. 'All right, this is it. See if you can slow us down as we make our approach. Weather permitting, we'll have outmanoeuvred the storm.'

'Ay, sir!'

Thunder cracked loudly, reverberating in Edmund's chest. Lightning lit up the way ahead and Edmund saw just enough of a glint to realise that if they continued on this course, they would hit large rocks that sat hidden just beneath the water's surface.

Edmund shouted to his crew. 'Collision ahead! Turn port! Now!'

But it was too late. A wave shoved the ship forward and it crashed down with a loud crack onto one of the many hidden rocks that stretched out far into the ocean. The ship seesawed.

Edmund grabbed onto the mast for support as many crew members fell onto the tilting deck. A shrill cry stilled his heart and drew his attention away from the rocks and to Amelia. The ship careened as it rolled on the roiling waves and there was nothing that could stop its ever tilting momentum.

Edmund sprang forward, grabbing Amelia as she nearly fell backwards – she would have fallen overboard. He held her close to his chest.

'I've got you,' he whispered.

Edmund held Amelia ever tightly, scanning frantically for Chuk, his first mate, and his best mate. He was relieved when he saw the Nigerian pirate hanging from one of the rafters.

The last time Edmund had been caught in such a devastating storm, William had been with him. The two of them had worked diligently to ensure all the cargo was secure and the crew safe before things had become too unmanageable.

Edmund's heart stung – William might have abandoned him, but he had not abandoned William. Even now he hoped Willliam would retrieve what Edmund had left behind at the port for him. Again Edmund was brought back to the past.

* * *

Everyone on the *Charming Trove* knew William was Edmund's brother, his junior by only three years, despite their father treating them as though they were a decade apart. When William left, he formed his own band of pirates and told none that Edmund was his brother. William began denying the reasons why he had left the crew.

Perhaps William was right, for so much had he been in Edmund's shadow that none of the other pirates knew they were brothers. They'd get remarks that they looked alike and folks asked if they were related, but it was not widespread knowledge. However, after William left Edmund's side, it became known among all pirates that Edmund was the younger man's rival and William wanted nothing to do with him or his crew. It stung, every day.

When Edmund walked into the tavern, he maintained the appearance of a fierce Captain, even if he felt frail without his brother by his side.

'What's this?' the barkeep asked.

'You are to pass this on to Captain William, at all costs.' Edmund slid gold doubloons onto the counter. 'I trust you will see this task done, or I will hunt you down, I swear it.'

'Is this a trap for your rival?' The barkeep took the gold and the glass cylinder.

'It is a challenge. He is to take it up and meet with me as per my instructions contained within.' He leaned forward and lowered his voice. 'If you speak of this to any other pirate or fail to deliver it, or take a peek inside, I will know, and the consequences will be severe, you hear me?'

'Ay, sir!'

Edmund's reputation for going after any and all who wronged or deceived him preceded him, thankfully, and he trusted the barkeep would pass on the cylinder to William. What the younger man did with it afterwards was up to him.

* * *

And now, as Edmund hung for dear life, muscles straining and aching, he hoped, whatever happened to him, William would find him.

The ship bucked back into place. Edmund cleared his throat, taking a step away from Amelia, feeling his cheeks flush as heat rose to his face.

'As you were.'

Edmund scanned the deck, assessing the damage. Lightning crackled overhead and another wave caused the *Charmed Trove* to slant forward. Edmund fell to his knees as the ship seesawed once more. He drew in a sharp breath in time before he was plunged into the water along with half the ship and crew.

Edmund swam out from beneath the ship, searching frantically for Amelia, his chest tight with worry. His lungs began to burn for air.

As Edmund began towards the surface of the water, something hit his head. He blew out a cough before his vision blurred and he was pulled into darkness.

PART TWO

The *Tame Dame* anchored at Port Barnache. William walked off the deck and dipped his head, holding the tip of his hat to the port's guard.

'We want no trouble from you lot, you hear?' the guard complained.

William gave him his best grin. 'Worry not, comrade, we are but mere travellers here to purchase goods.'

'Yeah, yeah. Just don't get into any fights with any of your rival pirates and I *might* not report your presence to the Royal Navy.'

'Well met, sir, you have my word.' William put a hand to his heart and bowed, letting his hat drop into his outstretched hand before he rose and placed the hat back atop his head. He winked at the guard, sizing him up and down flirtatiously.

Oliver came up behind him, turning William with a hand wrapped around his waist. 'Will you stop flirting with other men, William!' Oliver pulled William along the dock. 'I want to be the only man you have eyes for.'

'Oliver, you *are* the only man I have eyes for, I promise.' William met his lover's gaze and smiled. 'But buttering up the guards does no harm.'

Oliver clicked his tongue, shaking his head. He turned but William caught his arm and pulled him in for a tender kiss.

'Oi! Captain!' William and Oliver pulled apart, suppressing chuckles. Andrea put a hand on her hip. 'Save the face eating for the tavern tonight. You're the one who said we had to be efficient, so stop wasting time with your tongues and be efficient.' The woman sighed. 'I tell you, Captain of the *Tame Dame* acting so untamed.' And she muttered a series of expletives in Spanish.

The three of them laughed as the rest of the crew joined them, walking through the port's streets.

William and Oliver interlaced their hands and continued down an alley, stopping in front of merchant stalls. Several crew members broke off into separate directions. Andrea and a few others followed their Captain.

William reached for a plump fruit, tossing it up and catching it again. He paid the merchant for many of the fruits and took a bite out of the one he was holding before continuing on.

'Have you heard?' a man in the street muttered to a woman who stood beside him.

'Terrible fate if you ask me, just like all the other ships that disappeared there.'

'Serves pirates right for chasing booty that doesn't even exist.'

William stopped, his heart skipping a beat. The conversation sounded too much like . . .

He turned to the two gossipers. 'What's this? Pirates chasing treasure?' He winked at them, plastering a wide grin on his face.

'Hey, you're Captain William from the *Tame Dame,* are you not?'

'I sure am! What gave me away? The neatly-shaved facial hair? My handsome features? Perhaps the emerald gems I like to wear?' William heard Oliver sigh behind him.

'Pay him no mind,' said Oliver, wrapping his arms around William. 'My Captain likes to talk himself up. Of course, I'm the only one who knows how handsome he truly is.'

The woman in the street burst out laughing. 'Your reputation precedes you, Captain William. The rebel pirate who rivals none but one other and walks around flaunting his lover for all to be heartbroken that he is taken already.'

'That's me.' William bowed politely.

'Rumour has it,' began the man, 'the *Charmed Trove* has finally gone in search of the Hidden Cove after years of boasting they would.'

'The *Charmed Trove,* you say?' William sought to confirm.

'Ay. And its captain, Edmund, was here but three days ago to announce his departure that very same day.'

'Three days!' William exclaimed, his heart dropping to his stomach.

'Are we to go after them and ensure we find that place of rare booty before *they* can?' asked Andrea.

'No,' William answered dryly. 'If Captain Edmund has three days hence gone in pursuit of the Hidden Cove, then he has undoubtedly found the place of legend. Good for him.'

'But if he's successful, his entire crew will become the most reputable pirates in all the seas!' protested Andrea. 'Edmund is your only rival. Why not best him where he's likely to fail?'

'Likely to fail?' William repeated questioningly. 'We don't need those treasures.' William resumed down the alley at a quicker pace, thanking the gossipers for the information regarding his rival.

'William?' Oliver's brows furrowed. 'It's not like you to dismiss such an opportunity. You've been wanting to stick one to Edmund for years.'

'The Hidden Cove is known for being a graveyard of ships,' William hissed. 'We are to stay away from there at all costs. I'm not going to set sail to the place where we might *die!* If Edmund wants to end his life pursuing an asinine pipe dream bestowed upon him by . . . his father, then that's *his* choice. He can die there for all I care.'

As soon as he'd blurted it, he regretted it. He put a hand to his face, shielding his eyes as they stung hot. He swallowed and took a deep breath.

'William,' began Oliver with uncertainty, 'in the years we've been together, you've talked seldom about Edmund, but every time you do, it's with the bitterness only a man hurt by another may feel. Is he . . . a former lover of yours?'

William met Oliver's gaze and cupped his cheek. 'No. Edmund . . . is my brother.' Oliver's eyes widened. 'My father chose him to continue where he failed. I was always in Edmund's shadow. I've not spoken to my brother in three years, since I left his ship. The *Tame Dame* is my home, she is my family now with all my crew.' He smiled lovingly. 'With you.'

William continued down the alley, without further discussion of his brother.

* * *

That night, the pirates of the *Tame Dame* sat in the tavern, drinking the finest rum the port had to offer. William was quiet and solemn, pondering his options. Something tugged at his heart and it bothered him.

'Why can't I just let it go, Oliver?' he moaned in complaint.

'Because he's your brother,' Oliver offered.

'I'm sorry I kept that from you,' William said after a pause. Oliver gave him a wan smile.

'Tore right through the hull, it did,' someone was describing. 'That was one hell of a storm, I tell ya. I do not envy the *Charmed Trove*.'

William whirled on the woman, spinning his chair, and demanded explanation. 'Why's this? What does the *Charmed Trove* have to do with any storm?!'

'You haven't heard? The day Captain Edmund and his crew left for the Hidden Cove, a storm hit the seas. Ay. Many ships came in next morn' needing extensive repairs. There's no way the *Charmed Trove* made it to the cove. There's no way the crew survived that storm in such wild and uncharted seas.'

William thought back. They'd been at a different port the night the storm hit, it hadn't been so bad there – the winds had swept the clouds in the opposite direction and they'd only caught some drizzle.

The dark clouds that had loomed in the sky and moved eastward had haunted William. 'A storm approaches, we stay anchored here and return to the sea tomorrow,' he had told his pirates.

William cursed under his breath. 'Why would Edmund travel in such poor conditions? He knows better than to set sail when such dark clouds approach. My father taught us both the same navigational expertise.' He balled his hands into fists, he hated that he still cared this much.

'Captain William,' the barkeep called out, beckoning him. William stood and approached the tavern's bar and the barkeep passed him a glass cylinder which contained a rolled map. 'Captain Edmund left this here with specific instructions to pass it along to you. A challenge, I believe. A summons, as it were.'

'Why?'

The barkeep shrugged. 'He had me swear to keep it safe and not take a peek. Said he'd learn the truth if I did and have my head.'

William thanked the barkeep and tipped him generously. The cylinder felt heavier than it should in William's hands.

'Edmund has gone to his doom . . . I will not follow in his footsteps . . . yet . . .' William sighed, resigned as the tug clenched his heart once more.

He walked back to his table. Standing above it, he downed the remainder of his rum and slammed the glass down onto the table. He glanced at Oliver. 'We're going in pursuit of the *Charmed Trove*.'

The tender smile Oliver gave him was all the confirmation William needed that he'd made the right choice.

* * *

William stood before his crew, looking down at them on the deck below, heart hammering in his chest.

'My fellow pirates, we're going after the *Charmed Trove* to find her and Captain Edmund. We're going to the Hidden Cove.'

'Captain, are you certain?' asked Andrea. 'What's changed your mind so suddenly? Just earlier you wanted nothing more to do with those pirates *or* that ship. Has your rivalry with Captain Edmund made you go mad?'

'No, it's made me see sense.'

'Sense? We don't even know where to begin to search for that place!' cried another pirate.

William lifted the map his brother left him. 'Edmund left me a map so I would go search for him. Somehow he knew – he hoped – I would join him. I was once a pirate aboard the *Charmed Trove*.'

'Still, you said yourself, the cove wasn't worth finding. Why would we pursue a rival ship?'

'Because that ship's Captain is my brother.' William downcast his eyes and softened his voice. 'I have to go after him, I can't let him die – or if he has met his end, continue without ever knowing what happened to him.'

'Your brother?' Andrea sounded dismayed. 'You never thought to tell us this?'

'I'm sorry. It was irrelevant, for we stopped talking to each other, we became rivals. I had nothing left to say to him or about him.' William drew in a deep breath. 'We have been a crew for many years but I have kept this secret from you. That being said, I will not rest until I find my brother.'

He plucked up his courage and expressed what he needed to. 'I will not blame any of you who wish to abandon me now. I may well be leading you all to your deaths.'

Unable to meet any of his crew members' gazes, William averted his eyes. He felt a warm hand take his.

'I will never leave your side, William. I follow you to whatever end.' William met Oliver's gaze. 'I love you, William.' He pressed a soft kiss to his lips.

'I hate to say it,' Andrea began, 'but I have nowhere else I'd rather be. Rescuing your rival, brother or not, that'll make you popular, and I want in on that fame.'

Others echoed the sentiment – none left the ship. William's heart swelled.

He called out, resolved, 'Pirates! We leave at once.'

William took the spyglass from Andrea as an island grew bigger in the distance. He studied the calm waters before them, clear and bright, reflecting the sun. Subtle wind rippled small waves. That's when William saw them – hidden rocks just beneath the water's surface, almost invisible to the naked eye. At night and during a storm, no one would be able to see these, and once they did, it would be because they were upon them and unable to navigate away.

Afar, near the shores, were many shipwrecks, vessels of various sizes, pirate ships as well as navy ships, all toppled over.

William directed the spyglass to the water again, the rocks were hidden again. Only when the light hit the water just right could he see these, and there were no indicators that they existed.

'Everyone who's searched for this place has come from this direction,' Andrea observed.

'These strange rocks afar aren't the only thing stopping vessels from returning safely, surely.' William pointed to several ships that looked abandoned and green with algae but otherwise undamaged. 'Some ships did not shipwreck, yet their crews never left again. We must prepare for the dangers this island might present us.'

William turned around and called out to his crew. 'The waters favour us today. An obstacle course lies ahead, we must circle the rocks and find a better approach before anchoring down.'

It didn't take long before they found a better vector of approach and rowed several smaller boats to shore.

William and his crew jogged towards the ship graveyard, eyes scanning the massive ships that had been abandoned by their crew.

'Captain, look!' Andrea pointed ahead.

William recognised the treasure chest-shaped figurehead of the *Charmed Trove* – the ship had been completely capsized.

William's heart sank. He ran towards the beach, rolling up his sleeves and removing his boots and hat. 'I'm diving in to find . . . anyone.' He let his belt drop to the sand before rushing into the water.

Several of his mates followed him. Oliver and Andrea remained on the beach.

William swam towards the ship, searching in vain for any sign of Edmund. He nearly breathed in water when the body of a pirate floated into his periphery.

He let out a sharp shout before swimming up to the surface and taking in a lungful of air.

He dove back down but only found pirates that were not his brother – they had been dead for at least a couple of days, all had drowned.

Back on the beach, William wrung out his clothes and secured his belt around his waist, rapiers on either side. He put his hat and boots back on, ready for a trek around the beach.

At least half his brother's crew was dead in the water – what a tragedy – but his brother was not among them – this gave William hope.

They found the body of a pirate a little offshore, ligaments torn from his stomach, and another several feet away, dismembered at the legs – flies were buzzing around the bodies. William clocked the strewn about weapons – whatever had attacked them had not been impeded by pistol or rapier.

Oliver hid his nose in his elbow. 'What happened here?'

'Something must've attacked them,' said William.

'No shit, William!' Andrea exclaimed.

'What I mean is Edmund would never abandon his crew for them to be eaten by beasts or . . . half-chewed in this one's case.' He prodded the pirate's body with his boot. 'Anyone know what kind of beast could do this?'

'Something with very large teeth,' stated Andrea.

'No shit, Andrea!' William met her gaze and the two tried to smile.

Something gleamed blindingly for a moment, William followed the reflected light and found one of his brother's rings in the sand. He crouched down to pick it up and held it firmly, closing his fingers around it.

'Edmund was on this beach.' It was confirmation that William hadn't simply not found him in the water, but that Edmund had been *alive* on the beach, or so William hoped.

'William!' Oliver called out. William lifted his head to where his lover stood. There were signs in the underbrush near the edge of the jungle to where people had passed, squashed and broken branches and plants. William nodded.

He slid the ring onto one of his pinky fingers, sighing, before joining the others on the edge of the jungle.

The pirates followed the trail into the jungle and walked for several feet before William found another ring, this one was looped through a twig.

'Edmund put this here on purpose – he's leaving us a trail!' William heard the hope in his voice. 'Keep your eyes peeled for rings, silver and gold.'

'Does your brother have enough rings to leave enough of a trail for us to find him?' asked Andrea.

'My brother wears fourteen rings on his fingers, two on some of them.' William smiled to himself. 'I always found him a bit gaudy for that.' He looked down at his left hand where only one ring on one finger he wore, the ring Oliver had given him, and slid his brother's ring onto his left pinky finger.

'Guh!' Andrea, who was several feet ahead of them, wretched and backed away.

Another pirate was torn limb from limb, guts hanging out, face contorted, and mouth open in a silent scream. Blood painted the jungle flora for many feet.

'What would do that? Tear a human apart without eating it?' Andrea looked like she was about to puke. 'You'd think this beast would want to have a good human meal.'

'I don't know,' replied William. 'As long as it doesn't feast on my brother . . .'

They came to a small rise, always following the trail left behind by the pirates, be it Edmund's rings, blood, or flattened flora. The pirates climbed the hill before stopping to rest.

William stood looking out into the distance, trying to see signs of movement in the jungle below.

Oliver wrapped his strong arms around him. 'We'll find him.'

'All my life I hated him, Oliver. I resented him. I mean, I cared about him, yes, but there was always anger and jealousy behind that caring.'

Oliver creased his brows in concern and offered William a wan smile of sympathy.

'Our father always ensured we competed against each other,' William went on. 'He treated us worse than his crew, said he didn't want us to think we'd get special treatment just because we were his sons.'

William pinched the bridge of his nose as memories flashed through his mind.

'He named Edmund Captain without even considering me. He asked him to continue his mission to find the Hidden Cove. Edmund kept saying he had to continue what father had started. I kept insisting that the dream had to rest with father's soul.'

'You care enough about your brother to be out here now,' Oliver pointed out.

'If you'd asked me three years ago if I loved him, I would have said no, because I think I was too angry to realise that I did.' William closed his eyes. 'Now I'm too scared to admit I always have.'

Oliver pressed a gentle kiss to William's cheek, the warmth filled William with the strength he needed to continue on their trek.

They reached the other side of the hill, came to a glade, crossed a river by means of a tall bridge, and still, there was no sign of Edmund. William's heart sank with worry. They had not stopped for the night, though they had slowed, for the tracks left behind in the earth and other signs were more difficult to see at night.

The gushing of a cascade filled the air with mist. William looked down at his hands. Thirteen rings plus his ring from Oliver adorned his fingers. The only ring Edmund had left was the signet their father had given him when he died.

William stared ahead. Something massive had come this way, the damage to the jungle was apparent, and claw marks slashed the trees. William unsheathed his rapiers.

'Be prepared for anything,' he cautioned his pirates.

Part Four

Three days earlier.

Edmund opened his eyes, squinting against the gleaming sun. It took a moment for him to remember where he should be and realise he was lying in the sand, the sound of water lapping on the shore just feet away from him.

He moved and immediately regretted it. He put a hand to his throbbing head and felt a bump – this was going to take a few days to heal, wasn't it?

Edmund was aware of voices nearby. 'Captain, Captain! You're awake!'

Edmund looked up at the smiling face of his dear mate, Chuk. The tall man extended his umber hand to Edmund and helped him to his feet. Edmund looked around, assessing

'Who have we lost?' he asked somberly.

'More than half the crew,' Chuk replied solemnly.

A knot twisted in Edmund's stomach. Clenching his jaw, he stared out at the ocean, at the capsized and destroyed *Charming Trove*.

'Amelia,' he whispered, fear gripping him.

'Up ahead, looking for something we can eat,' said Chuk. 'She's with the others.'

Edmund spun to face the direction where Chuk was pointing and began towards his surviving crew mates.

'We've rationed our water but we'll have to head into the jungle and find a source if we're to survive,' said Chuk, walking alongside him.

Edmund stopped and turned his head to his best mate. 'Who pulled me out? Someone saved me.'

Chuk grinned. 'You're looking at the very man.'

Edmund wrapped his arms around Chuk. 'I don't know what I'd do without you. Thank you for saving my life.'

'You owe me now.'

'That, I do!'

Edmund and Chuk reached the group of pirates. Amelia lifted her palms to show some berries they were enjoying. Edmund merely gaped at her.

'You survived as well, I see,' he said, trying to sound casual.

Amelia's face fell. 'Yes.' She blushed, then she scowled, and then returned to one of the bushes where she picked off more berries.

Chuk leaned towards Edmund and whispered. 'You're going to have to tell her how you feel about her before one of you dies.'

Edmund rolled his eyes at the Nigerian man who merely chuckled. He was right, though.

Taking a deep breath, Edmund began forming a plan in his mind. He placed a hand on the glass case containing the map, which was still secured to his belt.

'All right, listen up, we need to—'

A growl and heavy breathing interrupted all possible trains of thought. Edmund slowly turned his head to see a large beast that looked like a sabertooth – giant paws clawing the sand, sharp teeth in a wide mouth with long fangs, striped like a tiger yet shaped like a wolf.

Edmund swallowed hard, his heart drumming in his chest. He muttered, 'Very slowly now, let's back away, and—'

The beast roared and lunged forward.

'RUN!'

Edmund instinctively took hold of Amelia's hand and bolted it, pulling her along as he sprinted forward. Chuk with his long legs bounded faster than the rest of them.

Behind him, Edmund heard one of his crewmates scream as the creature gurgled in satisfaction.

Edmund only glanced behind before returning his gaze forward. The creature was busy tearing into its prey – perhaps it had found its meal. Edmund winced internally. He hated losing mates, but they had pledged themselves to his mission. Each sacrifice, each death, meant the others were saved, that was their maxim – it had been his father's maxim.

Another pirate slashed his sword and shot from a pistol at the beast only to become its next victim. The tightness in Edmund's stomach worsened – if fighting it did nothing, then their only option was to outrun it.

Edmund tripped and fell, nearly taking Amelia down with him. His hands sunk into the hot sand. If anyone was to find them, he'd have to leave a trail for them to find, one the beast wouldn't care for, and the rings that reflected the rays were the perfect items for that.

Edmund pulled off the first from his right pinky and let it plop onto the sand as he stood and continued after the others. Chuk had turned back to lift him by the shoulders but Edmund waved his hand dismissively.

'Just run.'

'I will not leave you to be that beast's fodder, Edmund.'

Edmund was heartened all while his fear pushed him forward. They turned into the jungle, hoping the creature would lose sight of them. Edmund took the second ring from his pinky and placed it around a strong twig. It would have to do.

Lungs burning, throats sore, the pirates ran and ran.

Another roar alerted them to the beast's presence behind them once more.

'Shit, that thing's fast!'

Running wasn't going to get them anywhere but killed.

He called out, 'We climb!'

Amelia jumped up, grabbing hold of a branch, and nimbly began to climb. Chuk followed suit on the tree beside hers. Edmund climbed the same one as Chuk. A few others joined Amelia and the rest climbed a third tree.

Edmund hoped against all odds the beast could not climb.

Only a few pirates were still scaling the trees when the creature reached them. It leapt at one of them and tore off his leg, growling in its throat. The scream that followed as Edmund's mate suffered a slow and painful death made him want to spill the contents of his empty stomach onto the pool of blood below.

The creature feasted on ligaments and guts, but it left the rest of the body untouched. It looked up at them, its fur painted red.

Edmund put a hand to his mouth, barely able to hold on to the branch that kept his balance. Chuk wrapped a hand around his arm and steadied him. Tears stung Edmund's eyes as a cold sensation hit his stomach.

Edmund lurched forward, bending and clutching his stomach, vomiting onto the dismembered corpse below. Breathing heavily, Edmund turned away, closing his eyes.

He didn't know how long they remained in the trees before the growling turned into a rhythmic pattern of calmness. The creature was guarding its territory at the foot of the trees – descending wasn't an option – but it was asleep.

Chuk made a few subtle sounds and motioned with his hands at the trees. Edmund nodded, feeling weak, but adrenaline still coursed through his body. Slowly and as quietly as possible, the group of pirates climbed through the jungle canopy from one tree to the next, carefully avoiding any branch that might crack.

Eventually, they were far enough they could move faster. As the sun came down, they jumped from the trees and continued on foot. Edmund continued to place rings on branches or let them fall to the ground below. When they reached the top of a rise, they looked in the distance to assess where to go next.

Edmund put a hand to his head. 'We need food, we need water. We'll die before that beast catches up to us again.'

'There is a glade down there,' said Chuk, 'we can rest there. There will be fresh water.'

'I've found some leaves I can use in a salve or consumable paste,' said Amelia. 'It won't taste good but it will help maintain our strength until we can find more food.'

So they did just that. Amelia's knowledge of healing salves and medicine came in handy for boosting their energy with little to nothing.

The glade offered protection and many smaller creatures roamed the night. If the beast were to approach, these creatures would alert them. They also took to cooking some of the rodents, finally being able to fill their bellies with meat – though Edmund had little appetite.

When morning came again, they continued on, slower this time, but at a steady pace. Edmund was beginning to run out of rings to leave behind. Two remained, plus his signet ring from his father. It was as much a burden as it was his motivation, the reminder of why he was here in the first place. This had been his father's dream, and his father had tasked him to carry out his mission.

Edmund couldn't help but wonder if William had been right all along, however, and his heart broke as a wave of anger threatened to overwhelm him.

'Edmund?'

Edmund met his best mate's eyes. The Nigerian man's brows were creased with concern.

'It is because of my father's mission we have lost so many,' Edmund muttered. 'Or is it truly my fault? Am I to blame for what's happened here?'

Chuk placed a hand on Edmund's arm. 'Your father bestowed upon you a title and mission he thought would bring you honour, would bring us all honour and renown. You followed the path laid before you, and we followed alongside you. We chose this path with you, Edmund. No one is to blame for what's happened.'

Eyes hot with unshed tears, Edmund averted his eyes and studied the map where he had inscribed his father's notes. They travelled for two more days, resting at night, before crossing a bridge over a river and arriving on the other side of a cliff.

'I hear the cascade roaring,' said Amelia.

Edmund spun around. 'That isn't the water.'

In the distance, moving fast through the underbrush of the jungle trees, was a large mass of copper and black – and from it came the heavy growl-like breathing of its hunger for carnage.

Edmund hissed as he hightailed it – everyone ran frantically as fast as they could. Edmund let a ring fall to the ground.

'Please let someone find us, please let this lead them to me, please let—'

His heart gripped him with a pang when he thought of his brother. He'd been so careless with him – he should have fought harder for him to stay. Instead, he let him walk away, had watched him walk away.

The beast roared. Edmund flung the last of his rings ahead of him, leaping forward. He clutched the signet ring. It was the only ring he had left, the only one he was not willing to part with.

He veered around some trees hoping to lose the beast, not knowing where the others had run to – they had all instinctively split off in different directions. Edmund hoped Amelia and Chuk would survive, he hoped *he* would survive.

A roar behind him and a massive weight on his back told him his time was up.

The beast landed atop him. It lifted its front paws and clawed at him. Edmund rolled onto his back, kicking the creature in its fangs. It closed its maw around his boot. Edmund backed away, unsheathing his rapier. He slashed wide and jabbed forward. He stabbed the creature but it only leaned back and pounced even more onto him.

Winded, Edmund swiped frantically. The beast closed its jaw around his rapier and flung it aside.

Edmund's breath caught in his throat as his life flashed before his eyes – as his failures flashed before his blurring eyes.

Hot breath on his face, the creature pressed him down onto the ground – Edmund felt his lungs tighten and was certain a rib cracked – pain shot through his side to his abdomen.

The creature opened its mouth, fangs ready, sticky saliva dripping down onto Edmund's neck. Edmund whimpered, trembling, and nearly shitting himself in the face of death.

'I'm sorry,' he whispered. 'Please forgive me, William.'

And then, from the side came a figure barrelling forward into the creature, two rapiers held high, jabbing again and again, in its heart, in its stomach, in its neck. The creature barely had time to recover before it swiped a clawed paw at the man who lifted a rapier and hacked down . . . and decapitated the beast.

It fell dead, and the man stabbed his two rapiers down into it, panting, before he turned his head to meet Edmund's gaze and smiled warmly.

'William?' Edmund let out a shaking breath.

William's smile widened. 'You're alive.' His voice came as a half-whisper, cracking. He took a few steps towards Edmund and offered him his hand. Edmund clasped it and William pulled Edmund to his feet.

Part Five

The two brothers gaped at each other for what felt like an eternity, eyes hot with unshed tears, and then finally lunged forward, arms outstretched, and embraced for the first time in three years.

'I am so relieved you're alive,' William wept.

'You came out here to find me? You answered my summons,' cried Edmund, weeping.

'Yes! When I heard the *Charming Trove* had gone missing . . .'

Edmund pulled away and stared at William with his sea green eyes, as William stared back with sea blue eyes.

Edmund pursed his lips. 'You want the glory of finding the Hidden Cove?' he inquired.

'Please, the only reason I'm out here is because I was worried about your sorry ass, brother.' He sighed, wiping his eyes.

'I didn't realise you cared that much about me. I thought the only reason you'd come was to . . . was because . . . if I challenged you.'

'You were always so obsessed,' William chided in a low voice, 'you failed to see what was right in front of you. I left because I cared about you, if that makes any sense, not because I don't.'

'Perhaps you're right, William. You once said you were in my shadow, but you always saw what I could not.'

'Well, you are shipwrecked and I have come to your rescue; I suppose this mission has become ours now. My crew and yours ought to find a way off this island, and see if we are truly that close to finding father's supposéd Hidden Cove.'

Edmond scrutinised William before breaking into a wide grin. He couldn't help but laugh and William joined him.

'You know, part of me wants to punch you right now,' admitted Edmund.

'Oh, *you* want to punch *me?*' taunted William, mouth ajar in an amused smirk. 'How about I punch your face in for your stubbornness in following father's orders and mission.'

'They were his dying wishes!' insisted Edmund. 'No, I'll punch your gut for walking out on me.'

'Oh, but it's a good thing I did, else I might've been beast fodder if I didn't first die in the storm!' William placed a fist on his hip and gave Edmund a pointed glare.

The two brothers failed to suppress their smiles as voices approached where they stood. Chuk, Amelia, and several pirates Edmund did not recognise arrived at a run and stopped short when they saw the beast.

'Well, you certainly didn't hold back, Captain, did you?' a woman with a Spanish accent awed. 'That *you* who killed it?'

'Sure did,' William boasted, offering a tall handsome man a wolfish grin and cocking his brow. 'I just saved my brother's life.'

'Oh, so now they know I'm your brother? I thought you had kept that secret.'

'He did,' the attractive man said, 'until a few days ago.'

Amelia rushed to Edmund and wrapped her arms around him. 'Thank the seven seas you're safe!' She pulled away, blushing. 'I mean . . .'

'Me too.' Edmund yearned for her, yet could not bring himself to say anything more as she took a self-conscious step back.

'William!' Chuk guffawed. The Nigerian man wrapped his muscular arms around William, lifting him off the ground. The two laughed joyously.

'It's good to see you, Chuk.'

Chuk playfully bonked William on the head. 'I missed you, you oaf.'

'I missed you too. I hope you're not all angry at me.'

'Angry, yes,' Chuk narrowed his eyes at William, 'but glad are we all the same. At least *I* don't hold grudges.'

'Hey!' William defended.

Everyone laughed before the group quieted.

'Are you going to introduce your friends?' Edmund asked tentatively.

'Right!' William introduced the woman named Andrea, several others, then came to stand beside the handsome man and wrapped an arm around his waist. 'And this gorgeous man is Oliver, the love of my life.' William pointed at the various crew members from the *Charmed Trove*. 'So I want none of you to even *think* about flirting with him.'

Edmund offered Oliver his hand and they shook. 'Does my brother still give doe-eyes to the port guards?'

'All the time,' replied Oliver. Edmund chuckled. 'But I wouldn't want him to be any different.' Oliver beamed at William. 'He's perfect just the way he is.'

Edmund's heart soared. 'My brother has found love.' William and Oliver both blushed significantly, and Edmund cheered internally for them.

'Oh, right.' William held up his hands outward to Edmund, fingers outstretched.

'Right!'

One by one, William removed Edmund's rings and passed them back to him. Edmund placed each ring back on his fingers, glad to have recovered them all.

'You're lucky we all have keen eyes,' said William.

Edmund clocked the remaining ring on William's left ring finger and how his brother smiled fondly at it.

'Right, then,' began Edmund. 'We should press on.'

William patted the cylinder at his belt. 'I believe this indicates we should search for a crest in the mountain north of here.'

'Lead the way, brother.'

* * *

The pirates arrived at the mouth of a cave that stood within a tall mountain covered in trees. William recognised it from the descriptions his father had marked the map with, descriptions said to have come from the few to have ever survived the island's traps and survived the journey back.

Chuk bent and touched the ground. 'Captain, this mountain is a volcano. The earth here is . . . ashen. We must proceed with caution.'

'Very well, Chuk,' said Edmund.

They entered the cave, carefully looking about and turning around as they ensured there were no dangers hidden within. After several hours, they came to a narrow pass that was marred with skeletons.

'How much you want to bet this is filled with traps?' asked Andrea.

'No need to bet,' said William. Oliver peered over the edge of a tile. William held out his hand. 'Careful,' he warned.

Oliver took a small rock and tossed it ahead several feet where it landed on a tile. A large clever came down followed by spikes that jetted up from the tile in question.

'Well, that confirms it,' breathed Oliver.

'Any ideas how to get across?' asked Edmund.

Chuk bent down and placed his hand on the ground, his face hardening.

'Chuk, what have you found?'

'I believe we have greater issues to contend with.' He looked up. 'There is a tremor in the ground.'

Edmund locked gazes with William. 'Do you remember what father used to say about what's safest? Inside or outside an erupting volcano?'

'It's safest *away* from an erupting volcano!' exclaimed William, alarmed.

The ground quaked and pebbles rained down on the group of pirates.

'We need to get out of here before we're trapped inside!' cried William.

'All right,' said Edmund, 'forget about the treasure for now. We need to find shelter away from this place.'

The group turned the way they came and darted down the tunnel. The earth shook again. William coughed dirt out of his mouth.

The ground beneath him suddenly gave way and he was plummeting into a dank underground alcove. He yelped in alarm and heard Oliver cry out his name.

William landed on a pile of bones, already feeling the bruise on his ass. Someone landed atop him and William realised it was his brother who'd fallen with him.

William's gaze shot up to see Andrea dangling from the ledge as Chuk pulled her up.

Oliver let down a strong rope, but it did not reach them.

'Hurry and get out of here,' William called up to them. 'Edmund and I will find another way out.'

'William, no! I'm not leaving your side.'

'It's too dangerous, go! I'm not losing you!'

'I'm not losing *you*!'

'Oliver, you have to find a way out to safety,' William bellowed. 'It's an order.'

Oliver hesitated. 'If you die down there, I swear . . .'

William clenched his jaw as the ground shook again, longer this time, accompanied by a louder rumbling noise that did not sound like the quake alone.

'I love you, Oliver.'

Oliver did not reply but turned his pained face away. William felt a pang.

'If anything should happen to me, Chuk,' Edmund called up, 'you have the ship, or, well, the crew.'

'Ay, my friend. But we will find a way to get you out of there.'

With that, the pirates left the hold above in pursuit of safety, leaving William and Edmund alone.

William put a hand to his mouth.

'You'll be reunited, don't worry.' Edmund's voice was soothing.

'You're one to talk. Like you're not terrified for Amelia's safety,' retorted William. 'I see the way the two of you look at each other. Just tell her how you feel already. You'd think in the three years I've been gone you'd have made a move. I'm surprised she hasn't moved on yet to someone . . . more . . . put together.'

'Oh, I'm not put together, now?' Edmund chided, looking vexed. He failed at suppressing a small laugh.

William shook his head. 'Come on, brother. Let's find a way out of here.' He turned to go.

Edmund caught his arm. 'William, wait. Please!' William heard the sadness in his brother's voice. He turned to face him. 'William, I . . . I'm sorry I never came after you when you left. I'm sorry I let you go.' William's heart tugged with old wounds. 'And I'm sorry I never stood up for you more to father.'

'You stood up for me plenty, Edmund. Don't think I never overheard the arguments and quarrels you and father had because of it. I know you did your best.'

'But you're right, you were always in my shadow, no matter how hard we both tried.'

'Father was a stubborn man,' William said, his voice low. He averted his gaze. 'I'm sorry too, Edmund. I'm sorry I left and abandoned you.'

'It hurt, but what hurt more was learning I was your rival, that you wanted nothing to do with me.' Edmund downcast his eyes.

'I'm sorry. I couldn't stay and live the life that father had dictated for us.' William pointed at himself vehemently. 'I wanted to live *my* life. And I wanted to leave everything he commanded of us behind.'

Edmund locked eyes with William and placed his hands on his shoulders. 'I know.' He lifted his hand, gazing upon their father's signet ring. 'It just felt . . . like I had to. It's how he raised us, to be obedient sons and do as he bid, so he could be proud of us.'

'That was his navy training doing that.'

'Training that allowed him to survive many perils before and after he became a pirate,' insisted Edmund.

'Perhaps, but it was also that training and the obedience the navy expected of him that got him and those whose lives he saved to be marked as deserters to be tried and hanged!'

'It was the only way he knew how to train us to be as good as him – to be able to fight like a navy officer and sail like a pirate,' Edmund concluded

The brothers grew quiet.

'He's gone, though, now,' William said gently, placing a hand on Edmund's arm. 'We're no longer obliged.' William sighed. 'I know he loved us in his own way. When mother died . . . that's when it all began – he wanted to protect us, wanted us to earn a good name for ourselves. I think that's why he pushed us, but in the process, he pushed us too far, and pushed us apart . . . from him and from each other.'

Edmund scratched the side of his neck and closed his eyes. 'Do you forgive me? Or do you resent me?'

'Edmund,' William began, 'I resent you, but that doesn't mean I don't forgive you or won't *stop* resenting you. First, let's get out of here, then we can rehash over rum and let it all out while we're drunk.'

He offered Edmund one of his signature smiles, the kind that he reserved only for those he *wasn't* flirting with. Edmund relented with a grin. The two backed away from each other.

'I believe I feel wind coming from that direction,' said Edmund. The two nodded.

It wasn't long before they came round a bend and were walking up a steep slant. The pathway crunched beneath their feet, as old bones rolled out. Many of the dead here seemed of various cultures – some skeletons had armour and axes or swords, others had spears. William shuddered at the thought of it all, pirates and explorers dying on an island such as this, in a cave such as this.

He heard the others nearing and the two brothers called out excitedly.

Before they reached the top, the ground quaked again and many boulders fell all around them. William braced himself as he fell to his hands and knees. A piercing pain tore through him and he screamed in agony, falling onto his back.

* * *

When the dust settled, Edmund turned to see William quivering on the ground, blood gushing out of his side where a stake had impaled him.

PART SIX

Edmund fell to his knees at his brother's side, gently taking his head into his lap as William's blood spilled from his wound, drenching his clothes. William was struggling against the pain.

Edmund's tears fell freely, he wasn't even trying to hide his sorrow.

'This is all my fault. Had I not been so obsessed, had I not come out here, you'd be . . . alive.'

'Perhaps, but . . . we still . . . wouldn't be . . . talking,' William managed.

'I'm so sorry.'

'I'm not.' William reached a bloodied hand towards Edmund's face. 'I love you, brother.' His hand fell and William's head lolled back.

'No, no, no!' Edmund quavered. 'William? Damnation! Stay with me!'

'There they are!' Chuk shouted.

'William!' cried Oliver, skidding to a stop and dropping to his knees. He looked up at Edmund across from him. 'What happened?'

'The boulders . . .' was all Edmund could manage. He shut his eyes as a desperate wail escaped Oliver.

'He's going to live!' declared Amelia. 'Chuk, carry him out of here. We need to find a place we can hide from the eruption without any cave-ins.'

The group of pirates ran towards the exit as the ground continued to quake beneath them. Edmund's heart hammered in his chest. The volcano was preparing but its eruption had not yet begun.

Oliver and Amelia worked on patching William up as the group paused right outside the mouth of the cave to reorient. Amelia fed her concoctions to William to keep him alive.

'Chuk, how long do we have?' asked Edmund.

'If we keep running, we could reach that mountain range there,' Chuk pointed east.

'That's perfect. My father's map indicates a cave at its top. We'll be well sheltered.'

'That's *if* we can make it,' muttered Andrea.

The pirates gave it their all as they scaled at a run to the next mountain range.

William moaned in pain and mumbled inaudibly several times but never regained consciousness.

Edmund realised he was trembling when they stopped at the top and slowed their pace.

'We need to remove this stake,' said Amelia.

An explosion and the darkening sky told Edmund the eruption had begun.

'We need to find that cave before any fire rains down on us!' cried Oliver.

'I'll scout ahead,' declared Chuk.

He gently placed William on the ground before bounding ahead at great speed. Oliver placed a trembling hand on William's chest.

'Hold on, my love, my sweet William, just hold on. For me. For us.' He shut his eyes, sobbing.

Amelia placed her hand on William's side and the other on the stake. She breathed slowly before pulling out the wooden weapon with a slow squidge. William coughed and blood spurted from the wound.

Oliver clamped his hand to his mouth as another sob escaped him, turning his face away.

'Are you certain he'll survive?' Edmund asked Amelia.

'I promise!'

Amelia poured alcohol onto the wound before she began lathering her salve onto it. Another explosion and a whistle in the hot air told Edmund time was running out.

Oliver took hold of William's hand, his face streaked with tears. 'Amelia, thank you for your efforts.'

'I'm a damned good nurse, Oliver. I've healed worse wounds on soldiers and pirates alike.' She offered Oliver a sympathetic smile. 'Used to be a Royal Navy nurse before my captain showed his corrupt side and I fled. But I've seen much carnage and death, and stopped a lot more of it with my skills.'

Oliver nodded absently before he sobbed again. 'I love him more than anything.'

It was heartbreaking to watch Oliver break down like that, and all Edmund wanted to do was break down with him.

The sound of hurried steps announced Chuk's return. 'This way!'

The pirates gently lifted William. The earth quaked again and Edmund nearly fell. Chuk held him up by the arm as Oliver followed, weeping, and curled in on himself. Edmund steeled himself and motioned his head to Oliver.

Chuk went to the younger man's side and helped him run, lending him his strength. Edmund raced towards the cave. It was on the side of a cliff that climbed to another higher mountain range juxtaposed to this one – its mouth faced away from the volcano, so they would be safe within it.

Inside, the air was fresher and calm, and further down, there was a pond that shimmered with luminescence despite the darkness of the cave around it.

They lay William down beside the water. Amelia continued to tend to William's wound and to feed him her special herbs, placing a cloth of cold water on his forehead.

'He's burning up, his body is fighting. This will help.'

Edmund watched as Amelia poured water on William's wound and cleaned it anew before she began stitching and bandaging it.

'All right, listen up!' Edmund called out, his voice cracking. He swallowed and balled his hands to regain control of himself. 'We settle here and weather the storm from here, we wait for the eruption to end. Stay alert. If the air becomes hot and stagnant, we'll need to move out, but this cave should provide enough shelter to wait it out.'

Oliver lay down beside William, interlacing their hands and bringing them to his heart. Edmund joined them, sitting down on his brother's other side and resting his back against the cave's wall.

Outside, the eruption rumbled, muffled by the cave's damp walls, lulling everyone to silence. Feeling fatigue overtake him, Edmund closed his eyes.

* * *

William gasped as his eyes shot open – pain jabbed through his side.

'William!'

Before William could process, the sweet taste of Oliver's lips was on his, mixed with the saltiness of tears, immediately stealing his breath as he deepened the kiss. William's stomach fluttered and he moaned when his lover pulled away.

'You're awake!' It was Edmund who voiced the awestruck statement.

William felt himself blush. 'A bit weak, but— I'm . . . alive?' he amazed.

'I told you I'm a damn fine nurse,' said Amelia.

Oliver laughed tearfully as Edmund helped William sit up. William winced at the pain.

'How?' he asked.

'The wound wasn't deep, merely wide enough for you to lose enough blood to lose consciousness,' explained Amelia. 'That stake, those skeletons . . . they'd been there for centuries at least. There was infection, which I cleaned.'

William reached a hand to hers and squeezed. 'Thank you.' William glanced at his brother. 'Though, something tells me you didn't save my life just for *my* sake.'

Amelia blushed and William chuckled. The woman pulled away, standing.

'I'm so relieved,' voiced Edmund. 'You have no idea how much I hated myself for what happened to you.'

'It's all right, brother.'

Edmund nodded, rising to his feet. He walked to Amelia – William watched the exchange, holding Oliver's hand close to his heart, and feeling comforted despite the relentless pain that shot through him over and over again.

'Thank you so, so much for everything you've done for him,' Edmund told Amelia. A sob escaped him.

'I couldn't bear to see you heartbroken after everything the two of you have lived. I know what it's like to lose a sibling.'

'I . . . appreciate you.' Edmund's face hardened in resolve. 'Amelia, I . . . am in love with you.'

Her eyes widened. 'Edmund,' she whispered. 'I . . . am in love with you also.'

Edmund took her face in his hands and kissed her with fierce passion. Amelia wrapped her arms around him, deepening the kiss.

William whispered to Oliver. 'They've been pining over each other for years. It was about time.'

'Not everyone can be like you,' Oliver replied teasingly, 'declaring your love mere weeks after you'd met me.'

'What can I say? I knew love when I knew it, and that was before I had you in my bed.'

'Well, had you told me you loved me before you bedded me, I would have merely thought it was how you wooed me.'

'Then it's a good thing I waited to tell you when I knew you'd know I was genuine.' The two lovers chuckled.

Edmund and Amelia pulled away from each other, breathless.

'I have been wanting to tell you for so long,' admitted Edmund.

'I thought for sure you didn't feel the same, for . . .' Amelia averted her eyes.

'I know, I'm sorry. I've been a poor brother to William, a poor . . . lover to the woman I've loved that I could not tell her and you never knew. I wish to make up for it and be a proper lover to you.'

Amelia drew in a sharp breath.

'At least wait until we're back at the ship,' laughed Chuk.

'What ship,' another crewmate complained. 'We have no ship.'

'Yes, you do,' declared William. 'That's . . . if the *Charmed Trove*, her captain and her crew, accept to become part of the *Tame Dame*'s crew.'

Edmund beamed at William. 'I'd be honoured. I mean, if everyone else is fine with it.' The others voiced their agreement.

William placed a hand on the smooth stone and Oliver helped him stand. William realised the cave was calm – the eruption must have ended. 'We'll have to return to the Hidden Cove.'

'Let the cove rest,' declared Edmund.

'Brother?'

Edmund sighed. 'You are right. I've been blinded by my obsession to follow father's last wishes, but what I have found on this . . . misadventure . . . is more than I'll find if we go back to that cursèd place. I found my brother, I found love, I found . . . sense.'

William took that in. 'Are you certain, brother?' he asked gently.

'Yes, I am certain,' Edmund asserted.

'Perhaps father sent us here for both our sakes, then,' offered William. 'Perhaps he knew and loved us more than he let on.'

'Or perhaps *our* love, rather, is just strong enough to withstand what we've endured.' The two brothers smiled at each other.

Edmund pulled out the cylinder that contained his map to the Hidden Cove. He pulled out the map and extended his hand expectantly to William. The younger man took his map out and handed it to Edmund. Edmund then ripped the two maps in two, then again in two, again and again until only shreds remained, which he let fall onto the cave floor.

'Uh, we were going to use that to navigate back to port,' said Andrea.

'I have what we need to navigate out of here,' declared Edmund, tapping his temple with his finger. 'We don't need these any longer.'

William glanced down into the shimmering pool of water where obsidian gems marbled with glittering amethyst glowed. He crouched and reached down to take one.

'It won't hurt to have proof we were here. I've never seen such a rare mix of gemstones before.' William placed the gemstone in his satchel and turned back to his brother.

'We leave this island behind and father's dream with it,' declared Edmund. He stared down at his hands and then removed the signet ring their father had bestowed upon him. He took a moment to gaze at it. 'Goodbye, father.'

William watched as Edmund tossed the ring far into the pond – it landed with a soft plunk into the glowing water and sank down to hide beneath the obsidians.

William gaped at his brother. 'Brother!' he breathed.

'It was time to let go.' Edmund met William's gaze, eyes twinkling. 'Besides, returning from this place is enough to make us both lords of the seas.'

William laughed heartily. 'I will claim credit for finding and saving you, Edmund.'

'I will claim credit for luring you and finding the island, William.'

'And if anyone should ask about the Hidden Cove? What are we to tell them?' asked William.

* * *

The pirates of the *Tame Dame*, with their newest members, formerly of the *Charmed Trove*, sat in the tavern, recounting their adventure to the patrons who relentlessly asked about the Hidden Cove. *Did it have magical properties? Did you find the treasure? How did you survive? How did you get back? Is the cove real?*

Edmund and William exchanged a knowing look.

'We will neither confirm nor deny the existence of the Hidden Cove upon the island where we found each other.' William slapped the obsidian he'd taken from the cave onto the table. 'You may all fight for this. I value my life more than what this is probably worth, which is a lot.'

He stood, wincing as pain from his wound still ached his side, but it had by now mostly healed.

The patrons marvelled at the amythistic obsidian, and the tavern stirred into a brawl as everyone fought for the piece of special ore.

Laughing, William and Edmund – and their crew – exited the tavern. They draped their arms over each other's shoulders.

'Ah, isn't it wonderful to be back together again?' Edmund said fondly.

'It is, brother,' replied William. 'I'm glad we have become a team as dual Captains.'

'Where no decision will be made without the other,' stated Edmund.

'And both of us have equal weight and authority,' completed William.

'Because that's not going to end with them at each other's throats,' Amelia muttered to Oliver.

'We heard that!' Edmund turned as Amelia joined his side.

'As long as you let us step in when the two of you get out of hand,' said Oliver, 'all should be well.'

Arms still draped over each other's shoulders, Edmund and William wrapped their other arms around their lovers' waists. Edmund stole a tender kiss from Amelia, while William claimed a fierce kiss from Oliver, all while they continued towards the ship.

The two brothers strode onto the deck, followed by their crew, and turned to them, shouting out together. 'Anchors aweigh! Full sail ahead!'

The Mysterious Letter: Pirate's Puzzlement

William walked onto the deck, feeling the fresh salty air and the warm morning sun on his face. He looked out at his crew – *their* crew, his and Edmund's – and noticed an envelope lying discarded on the deck floor.

He scowled as he walked over to it. He bent, picking it up, and looked it over as he rose. It had no distinct markings, no wax or emblem. It was a plain envelope, but clearly, there was a letter inside it.

'Edmund!' William called out. His brother joined him.

'What have you got there, brother?'

William never took his eyes off the envelope. 'When did this get here? And more importantly, how?' They'd been sailing for days and had not returned to any shore.

Edmund looked up into the clear sky and shrugged.

'I know every member of the *Tame Dame*, and that includes everyone who was part of the *Charmed Trove* before they joined us. I know my crew . . . our crew.'

Oliver hugged William from behind, kissing the nape of his neck. 'You worry too much, my love.'

Amelia walked over, peering over Edmund's shoulder as he tried to take the envelope from William who would not relent.

Chuk and Andrea, who sat on the gunwale tying knots, called over.

'A flock of birds passed overhead not long before the sun had fully risen,' said Chuk.

'Just open it,' blurted Andrea before letting out a half-monologue in Spanish that made Chuk chuckle even if he didn't understand a single word of it.

Edmund looked over at William who finally lifted his eyes from the mysterious envelope and met his gaze.

'Well? Shall we?'

William sighed. 'Might as well.'

William opened the envelope and pulled out the letter. When he unfolded the letter, both he and his brother were surprised to see it addressed to the both of them.

Dear Captains William and Edmund of the Tame Dame,

I would like to colloquially inform you that I see through your game. Do you think none of us have noticed how the two of you built your reputations from despising each other before you seemingly reconciled? I know what this is. Pretend all you like, but the theatrics never fooled me. I knew from the start there was something connecting you.

By openly claiming to hate each other, you promoted each other, and all pirates respected you for your hyperfocus on your one rival. Hah, brothers, eh! And you think you won't come to hate each other for real, now that you both captain the same ship?

Edmund, as the older brother whose father had chosen as Captain, to relent sole authority the way you have speaks of weakness. Only a true coward would let another command his crew. I don't know how they do things in the navy your father left, but he would probably be most displeased.

And William, thinking you're so fashionable with a trimmed-almost-shaven beard. Why in the world would anyone relent sole captaincy to co-captain with his rival brother?! Rivals, my arse.

And then there are your mismatching outfits. If you have green eyes, you wear green, not blue and vice versa. Honestly, why either of you thought to wear the opposite colour is beyond me. If you thought it made you inconspicuous, you are wrong. I see through your game, William and Edmund of the Tame Dame. You wear each other's colours and always have.

Mark my words, I will spread word of your false rumours of each other, and your reputation will sink deeper than your ship ever could were it to sink in the deepest depths of the ocean.

Yours severely,

Carver

Edmund tisked a few times throughout the letter.

'Who does this *hombre* think he is?'

Chuk laughed at Andrea's remark. 'Someone who thinks he has the authority to speak on behalf of those who aren't members of our crew.'

'Sounds to me like he's jealous of your good looks,' Oliver told William softly.

'He sure seems to think he knows a lot about us.' Edmund scowled. 'And he certainly knows more than I'd like.'

'Nothing here is not already public knowledge by now,' voiced Amelia.

William folded the letter and replaced it in its envelope. 'We're going to find this Carver someday, and he's going to learn, you do not insult the Pirate Captain Brothers of the *Tame Dame*.

* * *

Note: *Carver began as a mysterious writer of a letter to an auctioneer in the 21st Century. Carver colloquially writes letters across time – he is a time traveller, you see – and he always signs severely.*

<u>THANK YOU SO MUCH FOR READING</u>

If you enjoyed this story,
please consider taking a few moments
to write a review on Amazon or Goodreads.
It would mean so much.

Thank you.

Please enjoy this passage from

STARDUST DESTINIES I
VARIATE FACING

The first book in an ongoing series of
Epic Fantasy NA Adventure with Romance books.

CHAPTER ONE:

The Departure

Niome Fairhaven was a young polc of ninety with beautiful long, dark hair that glistened in the light, and bright eyes of golden green. She most often wore a purple dress that her sorcery teacher Elina, the Great Wizardess of Teloria, had made her. She felt very close to her master, and now that Elina was ill again, Niome felt compelled to wear the dress, almost as though it would keep Elina on their earth longer.

As Niome looked through the ancient scrolls that she was studying, her father, Ceymi, bustled into the room. When Niome looked up and met his dark eyes, she saw the sadness upon his face.

'Niome,' he cried, shaking his head, 'it's Elina! She's . . . her illness, it's worse than ever.'

Worry fell upon Niome's heart, for she had been Elina's apprentice for over thirty years. Dropping the scroll she'd been reading, she brushed past her father and ran to Elina's house.

Everyone, it seemed, was gathering at Elina's door; Niome saw Gorthan the Chief, Henker the Elder, and Selemil the Governor among the villagers; even the tall Telorian who was her and her brother's sword-master was there. *They all know Elina is dying,* Niome thought. *No!* Niome could not conceive that notion yet – the death of her master, the person she trusted most and who trusted her most, the person who was the most versed in magic in Teloria.

Niome entered the house and closed the door quietly behind her, then walked into Elina's bedroom and stopped beside the bed with her head bowed low, trying to remember the few healing spells that existed.

'Niome,' Elina whispered with difficulty, 'you must protect the *Complement Book*. Do not let it get into Mirauk's hands. Teloria's destiny lies with you now.' Niome nodded. 'No spell can heal the curse that has been set upon me. Mirauk's evil was too strong for me alone to destroy.'

'I will find the *Book of Enchantment*,' Niome replied.

Elina smiled and whispered strange words in her last breath: '*Soû lagar andë roc, hëaûbo rede lari verei!*' And then she was gone.

In tearful sorrow, Niome bowed her head even lower, and repeated the words in her head several times to remember them. Whatever Elina said was important and had great significance, Niome knew that much from experience. Then she blew out the candle that sat on the night table. She knew what she had to do to bring hope back to Teloria, but first she had to go out there and announce the bad news to everyone.

No doubt there would be a meeting with the council, and a great gathering to figure out what to do, now that the wisest and most powerful of them had passed away. Everyone proficient in magic was asked to be present at the meeting, but Niome decided that she would be absent. She couldn't stand those types of gatherings. She wanted to be alone and do research of her own, especially now that she had a phrase to decode; that would help a lot more.

Niome left the bedroom and crossed to the door, where she paused with her hand on the latch. Drawing a deep breath, she swung the door open and walked over the threshold and outside.

A spiritual ceremony in Elina's honour marked the day when everything changed forever. It was the eighty-fourth day of the year, at the very end of Winter. The Telorians grieved for a full week before the council meeting took place.

They gathered in the Governor's Hall, a great, dimly lit room large enough to hold all Telorians, young and old alike. Gorthan the Chief, the Swordmaster of all Masters, chaired the meeting, which was attended by Telorians from all of the surrounding villages, even those from the far south and wizards from the far corners, for this concerned the entire kingdom.

Gorthan stood before the people, with Henker the Elder seated on one side and Selemil the Governor on the other. The great hall was filled with chatter that echoed the people's fear, but when Gorthan stepped forward onto a little platform, everyone grew quiet, their impatience and agony hanging heavy in the silence that invaded the room.

Gorthan finally spoke in a deep, loud voice. 'Polcs of Teloria,' he said, 'this has been a mournful time for us all, but we must not lose hope. I know that the warriors have been gone far too long for us to expect their return, but nothing tells us they are dead. Although Mirauk himself announced that he killed them, I am hopeful in my heart that some of those brave polcs yet live. They are powerful and skilled, and whatever dangers they face will allow them to thrive if they survive.' Gorthan paused, wishing he could believe his own words.

'If that is so, why haven't they returned?' shouted one of the younger Telorians, standing next to another young polc.

'Because they are warriors,' replied Henker the Elder. 'They are explorers bound to find peace.'

The boy gave the other a discouraged look.

'There is always determination and curiosity,' Henker finished.

'But what more could they be curious about?' yelled the boy.

'The land, other cultures, making allies. These knights know what they are doing,' said Henker.

'I know that!' the lad retorted. It was the same story that Henker told again and again. 'But what makes you so sure they are still alive?'

'Six hundred and twenty-eight years will get you far in knowledge and wisdom, young polc,' Henker replied.

The adolescent boy stayed silent for a moment, then said, 'Hey, I do know a thing or two about the dangers of travelling. I also know a thing or two about magic. I mean, I *am* a Fairhaven, after all!'

'Meysah,' said Selemil, 'everyone knows you are the son of Ceymi and Latua.'

'And Niome's brother.'

Some of the other adolescents cast annoyed looks at Meysah for his boastfulness, but the young polc next to him only smiled in sympathy.

Selemil continued. 'But you still have much to learn concerning—'

'My brother was the Second Captain!' interrupted Meysah. 'I think I'm entitled to my questions.'

'Indeed,' said Henker, 'indeed, and it is understandable, but you see . . .' He paused as the three leaders scanned the room for Niome to no avail.

Gorthan continued for Henker. 'All is not lost,' he said. 'Perhaps Elina left us, but her spells did not go with her. Niome Fairhaven was her apprentice and knows much. In time, she will become a Great Wizardess herself, so worry not for the future of Teloria – it lies in capable hands: Niome, for great magic, and Selemil, our wonderful governor, who has kept us away from harm for so long.'

Selemil rose. 'That is correct,' he agreed. 'And I have been preparing a secret hideout for us, if ever we are in great danger. So do not fear, my friends. We are safe from the people of Mork, as long as we stick together and help each other.'

The words gave the Telorians a little more hope. Their discord turned into loud rejoicing.

Selemil smiled and stepped forward. 'Telorians, your attention once more!' Their voices died down and they focused on the tall polc's long face. 'This won't be easy and it requires everybody's cooperation. We need each and every one of you to train as a fighter. Most of you have swords or a weapon of some sort; it'll do. We must band together and forge as many weapons as we can, but most importantly, we must rebuild the last section of our barrier, the wall around our kingdom, where I intend to put more watchers than before. Those who can see far into the distance will sound the alarm when they spy the enemy. *That* is when we will hide and wait for the perfect moment to ambush them.'

'How will they not find us?' asked an elder.

'With the little magic that I know, I will prevent them.' Selemil raised his hand, palm towards the floor, and jerked it. A hole opened up and a great light surrounded it. With his other hand, he pulled a crystal orb from his satchel and held it up. 'With this crystal, I can see what goes on in Teloria. And behold, the passageway to the magical hideout. An ancient spell from our ancestors is to thank for this.'

Everyone looked on in awe until, in a flash, it all disappeared.

'We must work in haste. Whoever wishes to assist me today, you may, but I only require your help two days from now.' Selemil glanced at Gorthan and stepped back.

Gorthan dismissed the people. A few hung back to help Selemil organise the remaining repair plans for the wall; the others returned home.

Though baby-faced Meysah was younger than his sister by five polken years, he considered himself to be much more rational than her.

After the meeting, he rushed home, only to discover Niome wasn't there, so he went to the Magic Lab. She hadn't been at the meeting and it was crucial not to miss one, especially in this case, especially because she had been the Great Wizardess's apprentice. It was almost a disgrace! He needed to find out why she'd been absent.

He found her sitting at the desk, looking through one of the books from a pile beside her. Meysah rushed over and grabbed the book from her hands. 'What are you doing here?' he demanded.

'What does it look like?' retorted Niome.

'Perhaps you forgot something?' suggested Meysah. 'Someplace you had to be?'

'I deliberately missed the meeting. I have no time to spend on anything but this,' she said, reaching for the book.

He held it out of her reach. 'Anything but what?' Meysah asked suspiciously, yet his interest in Niome's work grew as she explained.

'When Elina died, she whispered these words to me: "*Soû lagar andë roc, hëaûbo rede lari verei!*" ' Niome stood and walked towards Meysah.

'What, is that a spell?' asked Meysah, reaching to open the *Complement Book*, which had been left on the desk.

Niome grabbed it and put it in her cloak pocket, where the small book fit very well. 'That's what I thought at first, but then I discovered that the words were in the ancient tongue of the Kaulchèc people. How did I know?' Niome began to pace as she spoke. 'I looked through the language books and history books because I thought it was an ancient version of our tongue, but it's not at all ours. In fact, I read that thousands of years ago, the people who marked their place here among the Telorians, the Kaulchèc, knew great magic, which of course is why we know it here today. The *Book of Enchantment* was a gift from them, before they left.'

'I know my history, Niome,' Meysah reminded her, crossing his arms and giving his sister a lopsided smile.

'Then you know that they used our tongue to create new magic.' Niome picked up a large book. Not to be outdone, Meysah picked up another. 'It says in this book that our spells, our customs, came from an alliance between our ancestors and the Kaulchèc. So I looked in the *Book of Ancient Tongues* and started decoding.'

Meysah looked at the cover of the book he held; it was the *Book of Ancient Tongues*, an old book with a dusty brown cover embossed with golden scripts. He handed it back to Niome almost reverently, as though it was too ancient and invaluable for him to hold. Right away she opened it, sat back down, and silently continued her decoding. Meysah waited until she finished and leaned back. He looked at her with anticipation. Niome put down her quill, still staring at her page.

'Well . . . ?' he coaxed. 'What does it mean?'

'"*Under the Great Rock, by the river*",' she replied. Ignoring Meysah's puzzled expression, she continued to think aloud. 'The Ortim River has one distinct rock. It's huge, for one thing, and stands out because of the greyish-pink streaks in its centre. I think there might be something hidden there.'

Meysah caught his sister's drift. 'But the Ortim River is more than a week's travel to the north, and then we have to find the rock,' he objected. 'In this time of approaching peril, Gorthan and Selemil will never let you leave, let alone Mom and Dad.' He again crossed his arms at the mention of their parents.

'I'm still going. No one will stop me.'

'What about—'

'I'm going!' Niome glared at him, her mind set.

'Then let me go with you.'

Niome reached for her sword which leaned against a pile of books on the floor and slipped it into the sheath at her belt. Looking her brother in the eyes, she shook her head. This mission was hers, and although she wouldn't mind the company, worrying about his safety would only be a distraction to her at the moment when she needed to focus the most.

They heard the outer door open. Meysah turned around and Niome rushed behind the desk and stuck her head into a random book just before Gorthan entered.

Gorthan stalked over to the desk and slickly lifted the book out of Niome's hands. 'Why were you not there, Niome?' he asked in a stern voice as he set the book down. 'I am disappointed. Selemil was planning on letting you speak.' He waited.

'I apologise, but I needed to figure something out before it was too late,' she answered after a long pause. 'Look!' Niome showed Gorthan the notes she had taken. He studied them carefully. 'I believe whatever lurks there can help us,' she added.

'Well, perhaps once the repairs are complete we can take a look, but right now, no explorer can leave,' said Gorthan.

'That's okay, I'll go alone.' Niome started packing her bag.

'No,' Gorthan said firmly. 'There could be spies out there.'

'Then send someone to accompany me.'

'We need all our best polcs.' He turned to look at Meysah. 'Even our apprentice-knights. I mean, it's over seven days of travel to the Ortim River.'

'Not if I don't stop for the night,' Niome was quick to answer, her words overlapping the end of Gorthan's sentence. Even if he was the Chief, she knew that she needed no one's permission to leave. She only wanted the support of a trusted friend and teacher, out of courtesy.

'And then you'll have to find the Great Rock, then return to Teloria without running into trouble,' continued Gorthan. 'If all goes well and you find allies and explore the region, you could be away for several weeks, at least.' He shook his head. 'No, I won't permit it. It's too dangerous.'

'I can do this! I know how to take care of myself!' Niome exclaimed.

'Can you defeat an army of Morkans if you're on your own? You don't know what they're capable of. You were not on the front lines as *I* was during the Big War.'

'I won't meet any Morkans,' Niome insisted. 'I'll avoid them! I don't understand why I have to stay here. I can't do Teloria any good if I don't know what I should know. Elina told me that for a purpose! Why can't I—'

'I don't want what happened to Bahvley to happen to you!' shouted Gorthan.

Gorthan was right. Even if Niome was correct about the importance of Elina's words, Gorthan knew the dangers better than she could imagine at this time in her life. With danger approaching Teloria, there was no way of knowing what was out there or how soon it was going to come. Even if Niome had other authorities' consent, and even though she need not tell anyone her intentions, if Gorthan said no, it was no.

'You're young, Niome,' Gorthan said in a gentler voice. 'Even with what you know, you're incapable of defending yourself against an army of fully trained warriors – most of us are, alone. Besides,' he added with a sympathetic smile, 'I need you at my side. You're the one who knows the most magic.' He laid Niome's notes on the desk.

Niome remained quiet. She lifted her notes and sat down with a sigh. Gorthan stood silent a while, then glanced at Meysah, who had a sad look on his face at the mention of Bahvley's name. With a last glance back at Niome, Gorthan walked out. Casting a sympathetic smile at Niome, Meysah followed Gorthan out, leaving his sister to her thoughts.

Meysah woke at daybreak to find a note on the bed beside his pillow. He sat up and opened it. It was from Niome. All it said was: *Cover up for me; I'll see you sometime. –Niome.* Letting the note drop, Meysah leapt from his bed and ran to his sister's room. Flinging the door open, he scanned the interior. Though it looked intact, he recognised the absence of what she valued most. *She's gone.* He ran out to the stable and ran along the aisle, looking into the stalls. One of the horses was missing – her favourite mare.

He let out a long sigh. 'She can't survive on her own. I have to help her – somehow.'

Running back into the house, Meysah quickly gathered what he thought he'd need. Then he rushed up the street to Vigh Nimrod's house and hammered on the door until his master opened it.

The lean, rugged polc was one of those who had stood outside Elina's door the day she had died. Vigh was a tall polc, taller than the average Telorian and darker skinned, too, with a medium-taupe tone though he was not of Dûnelorian descent. He often wondered if his lineage dated back to a time before Telorians had lost contact with the fabled Kaltelians.

His pale eyes regarded Meysah and his handsome features creased with concern. 'Meysah! What brings you here so early in the day?'

'Master Vigh, I have a dilemma,' declared Meysah.

'Well, come in.' Vigh held the door open, then followed Meysah into the living room, where warm light from a lone lantern gleamed on the swords and weapons adorning the walls. Vigh barely had time to sit down before Meysah started blurting out words that didn't make sense, so fast was he talking.

'Niome wanted to go to the Great Rock but it was too far – she decoded words, so she had to go – because of the war. Selemil wouldn't have let her and Gorthan refused. We have to help her – she left me a note. It's dangerous out there—'

'Slow down!' Vigh insisted, brows furrowed with concern.

Meysah stopped. He was breathing heavily, out of breath.

Vigh smiled. 'Calm down. Start over – and please, speak clearly so I can understand.'

'When Elina died,' Meysah began, a little too slowly now, 'she spoke some ancient words to Niome, and Niome decoded them. That's why she wasn't at the meeting.'

Vigh nodded and ran his hand through his dark hair, waiting for more.

'They said to go to the Great Rock – the words, that is.' Meysah drew a big breath. 'Gorthan didn't want her to go,' he continued, picking up the pace, 'because it's too far and too dangerous and Selemil would never allow it. But Niome insisted, because she believes whatever's there can help us. She was refused permission to go, but this morning I found a note on my bed and one of the horses is gone. She's gone and she could be in danger and we have to help her to find out what's there!'

Meysah stopped and plopped down on the soft couch, his eyes on Vigh.

'Well,' Vigh said calmly, 'it looks like we have no other choice but to go and find her.'

Meysah nodded vigorously, but added, panic straining his voice, 'What else do you *think* we should do? This is why I came to see you.'

'Calm down. We'll gather a team,' said Vigh.

'But no big team. Not anyone who will bring her home without letting her see what's at the rock,' Meysah said. 'I know this is important to her and to Teloria – and to Elina, if she said it.'

'You believe there's something there also, don't you?'

'Yes.' Meysah nodded vigorously again.

'What will Selemil say?' asked Vigh after a pause.

'We won't tell him. We'll just go. Otherwise, we won't be allowed to go, and it's important that we do,' Meysah blurted.

Vigh looked at him sternly, leaning his chin on his fist. 'Okay,' he said at last. He rose and walked into the next room.

A few moments later, he came back out, now dressed in heavy garments for warmth. He swung a cloak onto his shoulders and pulled the hood up over his head. Then he walked to the wall and lifted down the biggest of the swords and attached its scabbard to his belt. Next came a knife, which he slipped into his boot. He looked at Meysah. 'Come,' he said. 'We shall see who is willing to come with us.' Meysah gladly followed Vigh.

As they passed a red-roofed house, Meysah halted, remembering who had stood next to him at the meeting.

'What is it?' asked Vigh.

'If we want a good team,' Meysah began, 'we have to get Jimmy to come with us. This is his house. I'll go in and wake him. He won't mind being woken this early; the sun is almost completely up.'

Meysah ran up the steps and entered his friend's house without knocking, as he often did. He ran to his best friend's room and jumped onto the bed, bouncing Jimmy awake. 'Wake up, Jimmesh! We have to hurry,' he shouted.

Jimmy reluctantly opened his eyes. 'What is wrong with you?' he grumbled. 'You're yelling loud enough to wake the town. You're lucky my parents are probably out in the garden.' He sat up and rubbed the sleep from his eyes. 'What is it?' he mumbled.

'Niome's gone!' said Meysah.

Jimmy's eyebrows shot up. 'Why? Where?'

'To the Great Rock to find out its secret,' replied Meysah. 'But she went against orders, so she's alone and we have to go after her and help her.'

Jimmy brightened. 'Are you saying we're going on a special journey? You mean, to save us from the enemy?' Meysah nodded. 'Well, why didn't you say so in the first place?' Jimmy flung the covers back and rose. 'I love adventure!' He walked to the window, saying, 'What's the weather like today?'

'Cold,' Meysah said almost apologetically.

'But it's Spring!' exclaimed Jimmy, sounding outraged.

'The weather is as unpredictable as the enemy. *And* Niome. Besides, it's only the first few days of Spring. Hurry, get your things; Master Vigh is waiting outside.'

'To go where?' asked Jimmy.

'I don't know, somewhere to find people who wish to join us.'

'Who wouldn't want to go on such an adventure! It sure is better than staying here and waiting to be attacked.'

'Exactly what I was thinking.'

Jimmy quickly dressed and the boys ran out the door and down the steps.

Jimmy's mother met them at the bottom. 'Where are you two off to so early?' she asked.

'Oh, hi, Missus Hochka,' said Meysah. 'We have an assignment to work on together.'

'All right, then. Just be sure to be back for supper, Jimmesh,' she said.

'Okay. I'll see you later.'

The boys joined Vigh, who was standing on the road, gazing northward. He looked at them but said nothing, he merely led the way down the muddy, snow-scattered road.

They encountered Lóim Weedler, who was Jimmy's age, two years younger than Meysah. He had been at the meeting too, but mostly to mock. He was a boaster who liked to remind others about things they could not have. Not that he had them either, but he pretended to be the best and the luckiest. He had always mocked Jimmy and Meysah growing up, especially Meysah.

'Hullo, lads,' he said. 'Why are you in such a hurry?'

'No reason,' Jimmy said warily. 'We're just off with Master Vigh on a patrol.'

'Says the polc with no master. Well,' Lóim condescended, focusing on Jimmy, 'I am going to train to defend the kingdom, and,' he looked at Meysah, 'I bet I could slay a dozen Morkans at once.'

'Really!' replied Meysah, nonplussed. 'I don't think so.'

'Well, I could slay more than you ever will,' Lóim sneered.

'I think *I* could slay a dozen,' stated Vigh, 'and if you don't watch your tongue, Mister Weedler, I could slay you too! Or at least cut out that boastful tongue of yours.'

Lóim shut up and left, his nose in the air.

A short time later, Vigh stopped at a little hut. 'Wait here,' he said, and went around to the back of the hut.

After a while he came back and signalled for them to follow him to a small door in the back of the hut, so small they had to bend down to enter. There was only one room, warmed by a fireplace before which sat a rocking chair. A table occupied one end of the room. Stairs descended along the far wall, and the young polcs followed Vigh down them.

At the bottom was a large kitchen and a bedroom area and another nook that seemed to be a storeroom for weapons. A short, lean, dark-eyed polc with blond hair, much younger than Vigh but far older than Meysah and Jimmy, waited there. He was leaning against a wall, smoking a pipe, but when they entered he pushed away from the wall and approached the boys.

'I am told you will need my help,' he said.

'This is my dearest of friends,' said Vigh, 'Boreth Culmik.'

'Hullo,' said Jimmy.

'I believe we have met before,' said Boreth, 'though just in passing, and a good while back.'

'Boreth has just come back from Telor,' Vigh told them.

Boreth nodded and shifted the pipe in his mouth. 'I've been there for a long while now, to help train more knights. It feels good to be back home.' He looked at Vigh. 'Funny how we change in so little time!' Then he looked at Meysah, and stared at him for a long time. 'Yes, I can see the resemblance – it runs in the family, eh? Adventure! Seems like yesterday.' His smile faded.

'What does?' asked Meysah.

Boreth smiled again. 'Bahvley, your elder brother, saved my life. I don't know if Vigh has ever told you the story, but I was being held captive at a Morkan camp, and Mirauk's best captain would've slain me himself, had your brother not come with reinforcements. My team, my captain and I came home to help save Teloria.

'This room you see here' – Boreth waved his hand – 'did not serve me as a hiding place during the Big War, but it staved several others, for which I am glad. I believe your sister hid here with a friend of your brother's.'

He smiled in sympathy. 'Bahvley helped many during his trip to Mork. I am gravely sorry for your loss, Meysah. I wish I had known him better.'

'Did you see him slain?' asked Meysah.

'No,' said Boreth. 'He went to Mork and the camp where I was held was too far from Mork to receive any news. Perhaps he was captured; best to hope that. I know you heard from Elina herself that she was told he was dead, but it doesn't necessarily mean he was.' Boreth frowned. 'But then again, if they say that Mirauk killed him himself ... Well, Elina told you the story, no need to rehash it.' Boreth paused. 'I owe him a great debt, and since I cannot save his life, I will save others in Teloria by assisting you.'

Meysah looked cheerfully at Vigh, who was smiling.

'We need no great army if we are to be undetected, as Vigh mentioned before,' continued Boreth, 'but we do need equipment.'

'We have to go see Gorthan,' said Vigh. 'He will be able to provide us with the necessary equipment.'

'What will Selemil say about all this?' asked Jimmy.

'We will first see Henker and Gorthan,' replied Vigh. 'They will advise us well. Gorthan knows that if Niome's gone, he can't do any more about it than to let us go after her. As for Selemil, he may have final say, but nothing can prevent us from going now. Selemil is a polc of tact but knows little of magic on the deeper levels, not like Henker or Niome understand it.' Vigh and Boreth shared a knowing look.

'I sense this may be a case where magic could be our only reliable source,' Vigh went on. 'Selemil knows that the wizards can overrule the governor's choice in certain circumstances. That's how it was in the times of kings and queens. Selemil is playing it safe, but Mork will attack again and Mirauk will use all his best fighters, those strong in magic. We will have to rely on magic.'

Vigh's gaze met Meysah's. 'We must follow our instincts now. I know in my heart that this is the right thing to do and you are our guide, Meysah. Lead us to Niome. She will tell us what we must do.'

They all looked at each other. Boreth put his pipe down on the table and started up the stairs. The others followed.

They walked for a quarter of the day to reach the large house Henker shared with his cousin Gorthan, on the other side of Teloria City. When they arrived, Henker was sitting on the front steps, holding his staff, as if he'd been expecting them. As they approached, he stood and led them inside.

'I have prepared lunch for you,' he announced. 'I knew you would be hungry when you'd get here.'

'But how did you know we were coming?' asked Jimmy.

'I know more than destiny itself,' Henker replied. He led them to the dining room table, where a meal waited. They all sat down and began to eat.

'Gorthan will be arriving soon,' said Henker.

'Henker,' began Meysah, 'I hope you don't think this crazy of me, but I believe that going out of

Teloria is a good thing. Selemil thought it absurd; that's why I mention it.'

'Oh, I understand perfectly,' said Henker. 'It runs in the family, I see, and I am happy it does. This is progress, I know it, and I know why you must go. You are meant to go, all of you. It has been foreseen.'

'Will we succeed?' asked Jimmy.

'That is for you to discover, for whatever I know now of the future may be changed by those involved.' Jimmy cocked his brow and slowly nodded his understanding.

'We'll have to word it carefully when speaking to Selemil,' said Boreth. 'He may get defensive about our safety.'

'Let me talk to Selemil,' said Henker. 'I told him I would have good news for Teloria that would seem like bad news to his ears. And he knows that when I do tell him, he must trust my judgement.'

'Thank you,' said Meysah.

'Hopefully,' said Jimmy, 'we won't run into too much trouble.'

'Oh?' chuckled Henker. 'You may. There is no such thing as "*not too much trouble*". But promise me this: when you come upon a grey house in the middle of a field, you will knock on the door.'

'What's in the grey house?' asked Vigh. Henker did not answer.

'I never heard of a grey house alone in the middle of a field before,' said Boreth.

'It's there,' Henker assured them. 'And you must knock on the door.'

'We will,' said Meysah.

They heard the front door open and close – Gorthan was home. He walked slowly into the dining room and looked at the guests, then at Henker with tired eyes. He let his sack drop to the floor.

'I didn't realise we were having guests,' he told Henker, then he turned his attention to the other four sitting at the table. 'You'll have to excuse my weariness – I was up all night. Remaining construction on the wall has begun and progresses rapidly; Selemil fears an attack soon.' He sighed. 'He's been fearing an attack for the past fifty years.'

'Have a seat,' said Henker. 'We need to ask you something.'

'Oh?' said Gorthan, sitting down.

'Actually,' added Vigh, 'we need weapons.'

'You see,' began Meysah, 'my sister left for the Great Rock, and I know she went against orders, but there's something there that can help us and we need to go help her – Elina told her about it. Besides, the Wizardess of Teloria can defy certain rules, even the Governor's, if she knows it to be good, and with Elina being dead, that leaves Niome as the Wizardess of Teloria.' Meysah wheezed to a finish, and Vigh gestured for him to breathe. Meysah drew in a huge breath. 'We thought, since you're the master swordfighter and a mentor to us all, you could lend us a few weapons . . . if you please.' Meysah stopped and smiled a desperately hopeful smile.

There was a long pause.

'Well,' Gorthan said at last, 'as Chief of Teloria, I forgive Niome and give you the permission to go. I can't blame *any* of you for wanting to go out there and do something. It sure is better than waiting around here. To be honest, I suspected she might go. That is why I insisted so much that she stay. Now that she has gone, it proves to me the importance of her cause. And now that she's out there, she needs all the help she can possibly get, as well as protection; it won't be long before Mirauk discovers she is in possession of the *Complement Book*. But I am not the ruler of Teloria and I'm wondering how to bring this up with Selemil.'

'I will tell him, cousin,' said Henker. 'He will come to see me sometime today.'

'Normally I'd be upset,' admitted Gorthan, 'but deep inside, I was hoping someone would be brave enough to step up and go out and do this rash thing. *I* can't because I have too many responsibilities here; otherwise I would have gone a long time ago, using all the skill in weaponry and magic I know. I don't want to waste time waiting for Teloria's doom, and who better to plunge into this affair than you. When are you planning on leaving?'

'As soon as possible,' replied Vigh.

'Niome was gone when I woke up,' said Meysah. 'She must've left last night or very early this morning.'

'Then we shall leave tomorrow, at the break of dawn,' said Boreth.

'Eat up,' Gorthan bid them. 'I will equip you after the meal.'

After lunch, Gorthan led them to his private chamber. He took out a box and set it on the bed. Then he laid a few garments beside it. 'I have been saving these for those brave enough to venture off,' he said. 'You have shown less fear than most, despite the dangers that await you.' He picked up the warm travel garments and gave them to Meysah and Jimmy. Then he opened the box. In it were sacks of herbs. 'These herbs will help you along your way. They will wake you, heal you, and invigorate you when most needed. They are magical. Take a sack each.'

When each had selected a sack, Gorthan set the box aside and gave Jimmy a sword and a knife. He gave only a knife to Meysah, who had a sword already. Then he looked at Vigh. 'This is all I offer. The rest you have, except this.' He took a smooth stone from his pocket and gave it to Vigh. It fit exactly in the palm of Vigh's hand, and gleamed ruby-gold. 'Keep this with you, close to your heart; it will bring good fortune.'

'Very well,' said Vigh, hefting the stone, which was surprisingly light. 'We thank you greatly.'

They started towards the chamber's door, but then Gorthan halted. 'One more thing,' he said. 'Prepare yourselves! Rest now. Clear your thoughts of anger and vengeance because if your minds are set on negative emotions, Mirauk will detect you and find you with the power of his mind. Do not dwell on him. Concentrate only on the *Book of Enchantment*.'

They all nodded.

Gorthan looked at them and smiled. 'This is good. May the stars shine upon you and protect you all.'

They saluted Gorthan and exited the house.

On their way home they met Selemil, who was walking swiftly towards Henker and Gorthan's house. 'Hello, Meysah,' he said. 'Hello, Vigh; Boreth; Jimmesh.' He frowned as if wondering why the four were together. 'Have you seen Niome?'

'Not yet,' was all Meysah said, but it was the truth.

'Well, perhaps Henker knows where she is. I've been looking for her all morning and I'm getting quite annoyed.' Meysah looked to the ground. 'Oh well,' continued Selemil, 'I will see you later!' He continued walking up the road.

Meysah and his three companions returned to their homes. He was packed for their trip and ready to go by sunset, and slept in his clothes.

Meysah woke early the next morning, so early it was still dark out, but he was anxious to leave and find his sister. He was dismayed when he found his father already up, and waiting for him. *He must have noticed the preparations,* Meysah thought, and wondered how to break the news to his father.

Before Meysah could formulate his announcement, Ceymi smiled and said, 'I've set your things by the door.'

Puzzled, Meysah asked, 'You're not upset?'

'Why would I be?' He held up the note Niome had left, which Meysah had let drop to the floor. Ceymi's smile never faltered. 'You have found the strength to pursue what I was always too frightened to do myself. I knew your time would come. Just promise me you'll be careful and if possible, to return. Don't let Bahvley's fate become your or Niome's fate. Return home after you have found what you are looking for.'

'I promise.'

They embraced, then Meysah gathered up his things.

'Good luck,' Ceymi said, and smiled again. Meysah returned the smile, then stepped out the door.

Jimmy was trotting up the road already. He met up with Meysah and the two best friends continued together to Teloria's main gate to meet Vigh and Boreth.

The officer of the guards on duty there looked at them. 'Henker has informed us of the importance of your departure. You sure are brave. Good luck out there. The Mighty Spirit alone knows what awaits you.'

'Thank you,' said Vigh.

Arrangements had been made to have their horses waiting for them, and Meysah found his Greyer there, eating some hay. Jimmy was given a horse, since he had none at home. Vigh and Boreth had their own there as well. They mounted up and urged their horses towards the gate where Henker was waiting for them. They thanked him again, and he simply smiled and nodded.

Outside the gate, they urged their horses into a gallop, and left Teloria City behind them.

<u>Also By</u>

<u>Also Written by Celinka Serre</u>

Stardust Destinies I: Variate Facing
Stardust Destinies II: The Drought
(https://binkyproductions.com/stardustdestinies)

Celinka Serre is an indie writer working in freelance and sharing stories of various genres, as well as anecdotes, on Medium. She believes in the freedom of creativity and always continues to pursue her dreams. Having begun *Stardust Destinies* at age 19, the novel series is but one of her many projects, being also a writer of fan-fiction, fiction short stories, various indie film screenplays, and a few collaborations as well.

Connect with Binky Ink:

WordPress Website & Blog
        https://binkyproductions.com/binkyinkwriting
Medium – Stardust Destinies Extras:

Medium – Main Profile
        https://medium.com/@BinkyInkWriting
X (Twitter) https://twitter.com/binkyinkwriting

www.ingramcontent.com/pod-product-compliance
Lightning Source LLC
Chambersburg PA
CBHW070411200726
48294CB00003B/1160